Contents

**COLOUR FIRST READER books are
perfect for beginner readers.**

To my double agents: Caroline Walsh
and Rebecca Watson – K.G.

To Lucy Napper – N.S.

006
and a Bit

Daisy had made up her mind. She wasn't going to be a girl any more. She was going to be a spy.

She had drawn a spy's moustache on her top lip with a black felt-tip pen.

She had found some dark glasses in a drawer.

She had found some secret spy gadgets in her mum's bedroom.

All she had to do now was speak in code. (Code is a special spy language that only spies understand. Daisy had seen it used in spy films; now this time it was for real.)

Daisy frowned mysteriously and crept unseen into the kitchen.

"Hello, Daisy," said Mum. "What do you want for tea tonight?"

"The ostriches will be swimming in tomato sauce this evening," said Daisy. (Which, as any spy knows, means "a big portion of chicken nuggets and lots of ketchup, please!")

Daisy's mum stared at Daisy and
scratched her head.

"Why are you speaking in silly words?" asked Daisy's mum.

"They're not silly words," whispered Daisy mysteriously. "It's secret spy language. And my name isn't Daisy any more. It's 006 and a Bit."

"And what are you intending to do with my hairbrush, 006 and a Bit?" asked Daisy's mum.

"It's not a hairbrush. It's my secret spy telephone," said Daisy.

"And where are you going with my perfume bottle?" asked Daisy's mum.

"It's not your perfume bottle," said
Daisy. "It's my invisible ink."

15

"And would I be wrong in thinking that is my hairdryer?" said Daisy's mum.

"Yes," whispered Daisy. "It's not a hairdryer. It's my secret baddie zapper."

Daisy's mum shook her head and went to find the ironing board.

006 and a Bit slipped invisibly into the back garden.

"Hello, Daisy," said her neighbour, "how are you today?"

"Good afternoon, Agent Goldfish," said Daisy. "Are your fins green or purple today?"

(Which, as any spy knows, means "I'm fine thanks, Mrs Pike, how are you?")

Mrs Pike stared strangely at Daisy
and went to mow her grass.

Daisy slipped invisibly across the
garden and went to give an important
message to Mrs Pike's cat.

"Meet me by the Golden Palace,"
she whispered, "and bring your
furry overcoat."

(Which, as any spy knows, means, "Hello, Tiptoes, why don't you come and sit by the shed? I want to stroke you.")

Tiptoes took one look at Daisy's hairdryer and skedaddled over the wall.

Daisy dabbed on some more invisible ink and peeped out of the garden gate. "No one will be able to see me now," she smiled.

"Hello, Daisy," said her best friend Gabby. "Can you come out to play?"

"The laundry basket is full and the big busy beaver has many clothes to fold," Daisy said.

(Which, as any spy knows, means, "Hi Gabby! I'll just ask my mum. She's doing the ironing.")

But Gabby gave Daisy a very
strange look and went to find
someone else to play with.

Daisy took off her glasses and walked miserably back indoors.

"What's the matter, 006 and a Bit?" asked her mum. "Aren't you playing spies any more?"

"No I'm not," sighed Daisy. "No one understands my spy language. They just look at me as though I'm silly."

Daisy's mum stopped ironing and put her arm around Daisy's shoulders. "That must be because they're not real spies," whispered her mum.

"If they were, they would understand everything you are saying."

Daisy trudged back into the living room and slumped onto the sofa. "Well they don't understand what I'm saying. There aren't any real spies around here, no one understands me and I'm not being a spy any more. Being a spy is stupid," she grumbled.

Daisy was just about to turn on the TV, when a mysterious-looking stranger with a purple moustache and beard poked his head around the door. He had dark glasses on, just like Daisy.

"Pssst," whispered the stranger in a deep mysterious voice. "Have you seen 006 and a Bit anywhere?"

Daisy stared back at the stranger in surprise. She put her dark glasses on again quickly and sat up straight.

"Yes I have seen 006 and a Bit!" she nodded. "That's me! I am 006 and a Bit!"

"That is good news," whispered the stranger, "because my name is 0021 and a Bit. I am a real spy too!"

"The coloured sprinkles will be meeting with the chocolate flake on the vanilla ice-cream at tea time," whispered 0021 and a Bit.

"And the crunchy cream biscuits and lemonade will be meeting

under the big yellow duvet when the clock strikes twelve," continued the mysterious stranger.

006 and a Bit frowned for a
moment and clapped her hands
excitedly. "Ooh goody! I know what
that means! We're having my favourite
pudding for tea and then a midnight
feast in your bed tonight! I'll bring
my comic and my torch too!"

Which, as anybody knows, means "Thanks, Mum. You're the best spy in the world!"

To Claudia, George, Lisa
and Mark – K.G.

To Mel, Jonathan and Jake – N.S.

Tiger Ways

Daisy had been adopted
by tigers. Her mum had
been stolen by a gang of
mad elephants, so there
was no one else around to
look after her.

"Come with us," said the
tiger chief, "and we will teach
you tiger ways."

"Excellent!" said Daisy, following
the tigers deep into the jungle.

"You'll have to grow a tail," said
one of the tigers.

"No problem," said Daisy.

"And you'll need to get some stripes."
"I love stripes!" said Daisy, jumping
over a small jungle stream.

"Where will I live?" asked Daisy.
"In a cave," said the tigers. "Caves
are the tiger way."

"How exciting!" thought Daisy.

"Where will I sleep?" asked Daisy.
"On a ledge," said the tigers, "or up
a tree. That is the tiger way."

"How brilliant!" thought Daisy.

"And what will I eat?" Daisy asked.

"People, mostly," said the tigers. "People or antelopes – it depends on what we can catch."

Daisy frowned. "People and antelopes?" She'd never eaten those before!

She followed the tigers deeper into the jungle.

"You know when you're
eating people and antelopes,"
Daisy asked, "do you have
tomato sauce on them
or do you eat them by
themselves?"

"By themselves," said the tiger
chief. "Tigers don't eat tomato
sauce, it's not the tiger way.
We eat everything on its own."

Daisy prowled through some jungle leaves and frowned again.

"I know what!" she said. "I've got a better idea. What if sometimes we do things the tiger way, and other times we do things my way! Then it will be much more fairer!"

"OK," said the tigers.

"So, like, if I'm eating people, I can have tomato sauce on them," said Daisy.

"Fair enough," said the tigers.

"Or squirty cream," said Daisy.

"If you say so," said the tigers.

"Actually, thinking about it, it's probably better if I'm the tiger chief from now on," said Daisy.

"OK," said the tiger, who wasn't the tiger chief any more.

"One other thing," said Daisy. "I'll only eat people that I don't like. Like Jack Beechwhistle. I don't mind eating him because he calls everyone horrible names at school. Eating him would be all right . . . as long as he's got lots of tomato sauce on him."

The tigers nodded and led Daisy to their cave. Daisy grew a tail and some stripes and began learning tiger ways. She learned to clean her long tiger whiskers without soap, jump from really big boulders, hide in long grass and catch and eat people and antelopes.

"Tiger ways are fun!"
roared Daisy.

The tigers learned to ride Daisy's
bike, eat jelly beans, read comics,
build sandcastles, watch telly, have
cushion fights and bounce really
high on trampolines.

"Daisy ways are fun too!"
whooped the tigers.

Daisy was just reaching for some more
tomato sauce when her tiger ears pricked
up. A dangerous sound was coming
from high up in the jungle canopy.

"Daisy, will you come out from under the kitchen table," said the strange and dangerous sound. "It's time you went upstairs for a bath."

Daisy crouched low in the
jungle grass. Just her tiger luck.
It was the sound of her mum.
The mad elephants must have
given her back.

"Daisy, I know you're under there," said Mum. "You've been under there ever since we got back from the school fête. Will you please go and have your bath and wash that face paint off."

Daisy closed her eyes and hid behind her big tiger paws.

"Daisy," growled her mum.

Daisy looked out from under the table and sighed. "Oh, Mum, I can't have a bath. I'm a tiger," she said. "Tigers are cats and cats don't like water. In fact, they hate water. Baths aren't the tiger way."

Daisy's mum folded her arms. "Actually, Daisy, tigers do like water. In fact, tigers are very good swimmers!"

"Not me," said Daisy. "I was
frightened by a crocodile when
I was a cub."

Daisy's
mum raised
her eyebrows
and then
smiled.
"I know
a tiger way!"
she said.

"Hot milk!" said Daisy's mum.
"Tigers love hot milk. How about
if you have your bath and get
ready for bed, and I make you a
tiger-sized cup of hot milk."

Daisy did a tiger tut and crawled out of her tiger cave. "Okayyyyyy," she sighed. "But you're going to have to help me brush my teeth tonight."

"And why would that be, Little Miss Tiger?" asked Daisy's mum.

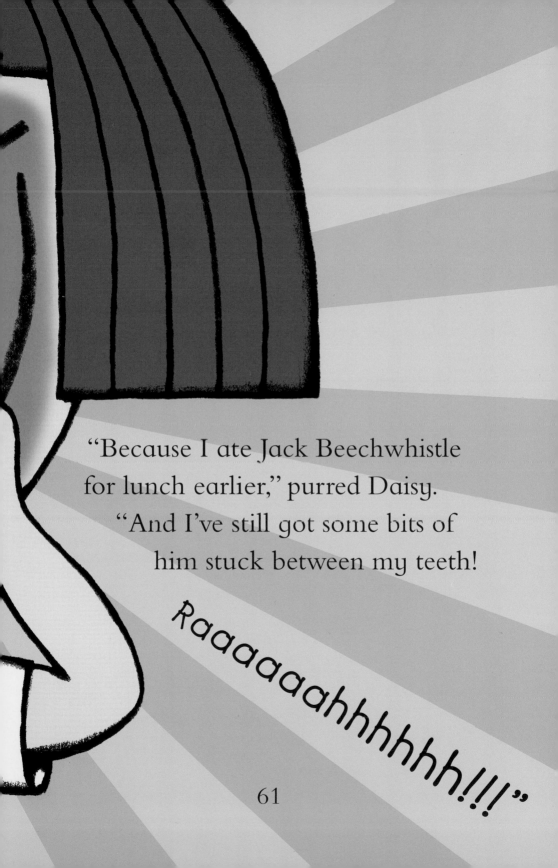

"Because I ate Jack Beechwhistle
for lunch earlier," purred Daisy.
"And I've still got some bits of
him stuck between my teeth!

Raaaaaahhhhhh!!!"